SECOND DANCE

ELIZABETH JOHNS

To Karen. For encouraging me to think outside of the box.

CHAPTER 1

*H*enrietta stared at the ceiling, trying to block out the activity coming from her grandson and his new wife's cabin. When she'd suggested them joining her on a trip to Italy and the Greek Isles for their wedding trip, she truly had believed she was a sound sleeper. She could not believe the energy youngsters had these days! Had she ever been so...*lively*? It was going to be a very long voyage if they continued at this pace. Three countries and thousands of miles, and there were no signs of slowing. Perhaps she would send them on their way by themselves after Christmas.

She threw back her bedcovers, deciding a walk on deck might make her tired enough to sleep. She donned her dressing gown and a shawl to ward off the cool night air and exited the cabin, careful not to wake her maid, Hanson, who was sleeping in a hammock nearby. Hanson was a dear, but she cossetted her and fretted as if a gust of wind would carry her away.

Henrietta inhaled a deep breath as she climbed the steps to the deck, and heard the ship's sails whipping in the wind. She was enjoying the sea voyage, surprisingly, despite the primitive conditions, and felt a new *élan* she hadn't felt in years. Little excited her at her age, and she pondered how she would spend her time now that Andrew

"

was married. She was too old to chase her growing numbers of great-grandchildren, though she would do anything for them.

She shivered subconsciously. She didn't feel old enough to have great-grandchildren. She had been widowed very young, and had put raising her family, including her son Robert, the Duke of Loring, above her own needs and desires. She had felt an obligation to help with her daughter Elizabeth's children after Elizabeth had died. Now the last of them had married.

Perhaps she'd continue travelling the world and stop wherever took her fancy for a time. She was considered eccentric anyway, and she was certainly too old to give any regard to others' opinions any longer. Life had become much more delightful once she'd dispensed with that inconvenient habit.

She leaned over the railing, attempting to feel the waves that sliced through the water and hit the side of the ship. She relished the feel of occasional seaspray on her face, recklessly enjoying the freedom of darkness too.

"Pardon, *signora*, please do not lean too much farther. I am certain it would be a pleasure to rescue you, but it would be very cold."

Henrietta did not bother to look toward the rich Italian baritone voice, despite its entrancing sound that stirred her curious nature. She did smile however.

"If rescuing old ladies gives you pleasure, sir, it might be time for you to find a new hobby."

She heard a deep rumbling laugh, and then she was compelled to look. It wasn't often someone dared to laugh at her unless they were family.

Her breath caught in her chest.

"You have not changed at all, Etta." He took her hand and planted a kiss on it. "*Bellisima*," he whispered.

She squinted in the moonlight, cursing her old eyes. Standing before her was an older man with silver hair, though he stood tall and confident. Could it be?

"*Luca?*" she said with disbelief.

"*Si*, it is I."

"Has it been…thirty years?"

"Thirty-four."

She subconsciously thanked the heavens he could only see her by the light of the moon. Perhaps she wasn't too old to care completely.

"What are you doing here?"

"I imagine, the same as you. I travel to *Italia*."

She nodded.

"Are you also without sleep?"

"Yes, I must speak to my grandson about his nocturnal *habits*."

"Ah, you must speak of the newlyweds." He chuckled. "That is young *amore*."

"Indeed." She nodded and looked away. "I did not realize there were other passengers on this ship."

"*Si*, I only came on board at Gibraltar. I have kept to myself," he responded quietly.

"Because you knew I was here?"

He gave a slight shrug of the shoulders. "I was not certain you would wish to see me."

"Dear Luca. Why would you ever think that?"

She searched his face as he pondered how to answer, and she saw the hurt still etched in his handsome features.

"It matters not now."

"It matters to me."

Why this reminder of love lost after all this time? She wondered.

"Shall we walk together?" he suggested and held out his arm expectantly, and she took it. "You are *fredda*."

He pulled her close for warmth, and she was surprised at her reaction to him. She was no longer a young vulnerable widow. She hadn't felt this way since…she had met him thirty-four years ago. It seemed like yesterday, yet, at the same time, a lifetime ago.

"How have you been, Luca?"

He paused a moment then sighed. "Well."

"You look well. Age agrees with you."

"*Grazie*. I think."

"Do you travel alone?"

"*Sì.*"

"You never remarried?"

"No. Only one woman ever caught my attention." He paused, looking out to sea. "And it was never freed."

Henrietta was speechless.

Luca continued, "And you? Did you ever remarry?"

She had known she had hurt him, but she had not realized how much. She had made the best decision for her children at the time. "No, Luca. I never did."

They both studied the sea and the bright starry sky in silence for some time.

"I have many nights looked at these very stars and wonder if you see them as I see them, if you ever see me in your dreams as I see you."

"Have you ever forgiven me?"

"Forgiveness is not mine to withhold. But I could never forget you, Etta."

"Thank you."

He led her to a bench that had been nailed to the deck aft of the ship. They sat in peaceful silence watching the moon and stars, and the occasional fish jump from the water.

"How do you spend your time, Luca? Do you travel often?"

"*Sì.* I travel often. I only go back to see my son and his children."

"I never knew you were quite so fond of travelling."

"I could not remain still after we parted. I believe I have looked all over the world to fill the empty place."

"And did you fill it?"

"No. But I have made peace."

"I never intended to hurt you, Luca. I was young, and did not know how to make everything work."

"You chose your children, and now your grandchildren. What will it be for you when they are all married?"

"Andrew is the last," she said quietly.

"The newlywed?"

"Yes."

"And now?" he prodded.

"I do not know."

He nodded understanding sympathetically. They grew silent again, and watched the moon fall beyond the horizon and the sun began to lighten the sky. Henrietta was starting to grow tired, now that the shock of seeing her former love had worn off. As she rose to return to her bed, Luca spoke.

"Will you come to visit my home while in *Italia*? There is no view so *bella* as *Villa Mare*."

"I do not know if that is wise, Luca." There were too many memories.

"We used to speak of one day making our home there together."

"I have not forgotten."

"There would be no harm for two old friends visiting again."

She smiled as she saw his face light up when speaking of his home. There were few places as lovely as Italy, she agreed.

"I would love for you to meet Giovanni and my grandchildren."

"I will think on it and speak to Andrew about it in the morning. Now I believe I am ready to sleep. Which is just as well, as I won't be able to look either of them in the eye."

"Assuming they leave the cabin."

"Oh, they are generally considerate long enough to remember my presence to ensure I am still breathing."

"Be happy for them. Time is precious."

"I'm delighted they have found one another. It is being obliged to share a wall that I am not happy about."

"*Buona notte, mia bella.*"

"Good night, Luca."

Henrietta lay on her bed, and though she was exhausted, it was some time before her mind—and her heart—could slow down. She had never thought she would see him again, and she was surprised how much his presence still affected her. She was too old for these feelings anymore. But what was she to do now that her family no longer needed her? She tossed and turned, unable to stop worrying. Her heart was pleading for love, but her mind was reminding her of her age and imperfections. Would it be better to hold onto the memories and move on?

❧

"It is three in the afternoon!" Andrew exclaimed.

"Hanson would have told us if something were amiss," his wife, Gwen, tried to reassure him.

"She may stay in her bed reading, but she never *sleeps* all day. I never should have agreed to go gallivanting all over the world with her."

"Perhaps she has been afflicted with seasickness, as we are."

"The seas are calm, Gwen."

"She wanted to see the world, as did I."

"That does not mean it was a good idea. I'm going in."

He walked out of their small cabin to the door immediately next to theirs and knocked.

Hanson looked out and gave Andrew a warning frown with a finger over her mouth.

"What is the matter with my grandmother?"

"Shh, Master Andrew. She did not rest well last night," Hanson whispered loudly.

"Let him in, Hanson," the Dowager called from her bed.

"Are you ill?" Andrew asked as he rushed to her side with concern.

"No. I'm only tired. You may leave us, Hanson."

Andrew paced the small cabin, worried. "Should I insist we stop at the nearest port for a doctor?"

"No, you fool. I'm simply not sleeping well. At night," she added to indicate she had been resting when he arrived.

"Shall I send for some brandy?"

"I don't need anything, Andrew."

"But, Gran..." he protested.

"Stop fussing over me this instant!" she demanded.

"But," he protested.

"No." She held up her hand.

"All I need is quiet," she muttered.

He pondered her statement then realized her meaning. His cheeks reddened.

"I-I apologize."

"There is no need to blush. You are doing what newlyweds do."

"You could have said something sooner."

"You are daft."

"And you said you were a sound sleeper."

"So I was."

He cleared his throat.

"All was not lost. I took a stroll, met an old friend, chatted, and then returned to slumber," she said casually.

"Pardon?" He looked at her suspiciously.

"No, my attics have not gone queer."

"You do realize we are not in London or Bath? One does not simply stroll and meet old acquaintances onboard a private schooner sailing across the Mediterranean."

"There is another passenger onboard. Were you aware?"

"Yes, we've met. A pleasant Italian count."

"He is an old acquaintance of mine."

"Is he?" He eyed her with suspicion.

"And when I could not sleep," she made a little noise with her throat and raised an eyebrow, "I decided to stroll on the deck for some fresh air and ran into him."

"You should not be out alone at night, Gran."

"I am not a young debutante, nor am I so old that the wind will blow me overboard."

"You mistake my meaning."

"No, I'm certain I do not."

"I collect you spent the entire night becoming reacquainted?"

"Not the entire night."

"I had better make myself more known to this count."

"Luca has invited us to visit his villa during our stay in Italy."

"*Luca?* You are already so familiar?"

She sighed. "I was engaged to marry Luca after your grandfather died."

"Pardon? I have never heard any of this."

"It is not something one speaks about. It was before you were born."

"What happened?"

"I realized Robert and Elizabeth needed me more. Robert was struggling with running the dukedom, and Elizabeth was making her debut. It was not the right time. The decision would have been a very selfish one."

"Do you regret your decision?"

"I'm too old for regrets, dear. I would make the same decision if I had to make it again, given the same circumstances."

"And had the circumstances been different?" he questioned.

"Perhaps," she said pensively.

"The circumstances are different now."

"Yes, we are both old."

"Are you ever too old to be loved?"

"I don't know, dear. I don't know."

"Well, I love you. I know it isn't the same, but please do not feel the need to run off for fear you are in our way. We will try to be more *considerate*."

"It matters not now. We are due to arrive any day."

"Where is this villa we are to visit?"

"Does that mean you agree?"

"I would not mind a few days on land. Besides, if you thought him worthy of a betrothal, I cannot object to becoming better acquainted."

Andrew had never seen his gran wear a smile like the one she was wearing now. It made him wonder exactly what he was agreeing to, and what his gran and this *conte* had been up to.

"I don't need your permission, you know," she said arrogantly.

"I know," he said solemnly.

"But I should like it just the same."

"I only wish for your happiness as you wish for mine. Are you expecting something more from this?"

"No, dear. He is an old friend. It will be nice to become reacquainted. His villa boasts some breathtaking views. Gwen will be enchanted."

"I thought you had not been to Italy before," he said, trying to remember.

"It was a lifetime ago. I'm too old to recall," she said evasively.

He eyed her and shook his head. No one had a sharper memory than her. There was a knock on the door and Andrew opened it narrowly to see who was there.

"Hello, darling."

"Is everything all right?" Gwen asked with concern on her face.

"Come in and see." He stepped out of the way to let his bride enter.

"Good morning, dear," the Dowager greeted Gwen.

"Good *afternoon*," Gwen corrected with a chuckle.

"Gran has been up all night with a man," Andrew said with a whisper of scandal in his voice.

"Good for her," Gwen winked at the Dowager teasingly.

"Do you think I am too old for a man to be interested in me, young man?" Henrietta asked, taunting her grandson.

"I do not think at all about how men view my grandmother," Andrew said with distaste and a scowling face.

Gwen clapped her hands excitedly. "I cannot wait to meet him!"

"He is merely an old friend, my dear."

"An old friend she was betrothed to," Andrew added helpfully.

"A very long time ago," the Dowager countered.

"Who has invited us to stay at his villa," he retorted.

"There is nothing suspicious about that," she sallied.

"I want to hear about your romance." Gwen interjected.

"I want to jump overboard," Andrew muttered.

"Perhaps after my tea, dear. If I'm not too old to remember any of it." She cast a narrowed glance at her grandson.

"Apparently the villa boasts beautiful views," Andrew said to Gwen.

"This keeps getting better," she exclaimed. "A real Italian villa. I hope there are rolling vineyards and turquoise seas."

"I am certain you will not lack for subject matter," Henrietta affirmed.

There was another gentle knock on the door.

"Enter," the Dowager commanded.

Hanson entered the crowded cabin and curtsied. "The captain asked me to inform Your Grace that he has caught a glimpse of the coast, in case you might be wanting to prepare yourself for landing in a few hours."

"It seems too soon to be arriving," Andrew said.

"Not to me," Gwen protested.

"I suspect Luca may have directed the captain to sail closer to his villa."

"Sounds like an excellent plan to me if we are on land sooner," Gwen said.

"I only hope we do not come to regret this," Andrew muttered to his wife, who promptly elbowed him to hush.

CHAPTER 2

*H*enrietta was not sure what she had got herself into. She had not intended to blurt everything out to Andrew, but it had happened. She watched in the looking-glass as Hanson completed her toilette, and she had to admit there was a bloom in her face that she had not seen in decades: she looked younger, and she looked happy. Despite what she had told her grandson, she did have some regrets. Though she did not regret putting her children first, she had always wondered what her life would have been like had she married Luca. She would have been happy, but it would have been hard on her family. She shook her head, to the chagrin of her maid who tsked at her long-time employer.

"I'm sorry, dear, I was thinking."

"About the handsome count?" Hanson prodded.

"Perhaps." The Dowager smiled. "Let us finish so I can watch us sail in. There is nothing like the Italian coast."

"Yes, Your Grace."

Henrietta hurried up to the deck, partly with anticipation of seeing Italy, but partly with anticipation of meeting Luca—if she were honest. The skies were clear and the sun was setting in the evening sky. The air was warm with a gentle breeze. She looked around as her eyes adjusted, taking in the brilliant colours of the sea, which ranged from deep indigo to aquamarine and everything in between. She looked ahead at the land, at the mountainous terrain and the cliffs, which lay in front of them.

"*Buona sera.*"

"Good afternoon, Luca." She turned to greet her old love by the light of day, and was surprised she found him to be as handsome as the last day she had seen him. It was not fair that silver hair and wrinkles gave a man more character, whereas a woman only looked more haggard.

He kissed her hand and a jolt of energy rushed through her. She felt a moment of déjà vu, recalling the night when she'd first met him in a Paris ballroom. She felt as if she were transported back to that moment three decades before. All of her old feelings rushed over her and she struggled to remain unaffected as he looked into her eyes.

His voice interrupted her reminiscing. "It feels like that night in Paris, yes?"

She nodded. He had felt it too. It was inconceivable that this was happening again.

"Do not fight it, *mia bella,*" he whispered.

She was not sure she could fight. Everything was happening so quickly, with or without her consent. "You still dare to flatter me?" she asked with scepticism.

"It is not flattery, only truth. There has never been another to compare to you."

"Who am I to argue?" she sallied.

"Has it changed much?" He indicated towards the shore, but still held onto her hand.

"It is just as I remember. I assume I won't have to climb that hill?"

He laughed. "No, *mia bella*, we will ride. There is a pathway from where we land."

"I am delighted to hear it."

Henrietta continued to survey the scene before her. The village was built into the side of the cliff, with brightly painted homes perched amongst the sand-coloured stones and lush gardens. She had fallen in love with Italy as much as she had Luca when she was last here, but she had never thought she would visit again.

"Gwen will not want to leave until she has painted every angle and view."

"*Impossibile*. That is why they say an artist in Italia is now Italian."

"I will leave that up to her husband."

"He will be happy wherever he is with her," he said meaningfully.

They surveyed the newlyweds who were also watching land approach.

"I agree. As long as they are together, it will not matter where they live."

"I have not been introduced to the young bride."

"We should remedy the oversight. She is delightful."

They walked toward Andrew and Gwen, who were absorbed in the Eden-esque scene before them.

"Andrew, Gwendolyn has not been introduced to Luca. Gwendolyn Abbott, may I introduce Luca Faranese, Conte de Salerno."

Gwendolyn curtsied, and the Conte bowed royally over her hand.

"It is a wonderful pleasure to meet you. I am especially grateful for the chance to see the *Duchessa* again. I welcome you to my home and hope you will make it yours as long as you like."

"Thank you, sir. We have to be in France by Christmas," Andrew reminded his bride.

"You must stay until the *Festa dell'uva*, our celebration of the wine. It will be at the next moon."

"I'm certain we can manage until then. My wife is beside herself to see your country," Andrew assured him.

"It has long been a dream of mine," Gwen said to the Conte.

"I hope all of your dreams will be fulfilled. If I may be of service, you need only ask."

"You are very good, sir."

"What do you think thus far?"

"I had envisioned sandy beaches and rolling hills covered with vineyards. Or a city on canals as I have seen in paintings. This is very mountainous."

"*Si*, not all of Italy looks like *Venezia*. There are many volcanoes and mountains in this region. To the north, there are rolling hills. It is a land of many faces."

"I see that," Gwen said admiringly. "How far is your home?"

"Not far at all." He looked up to the top of one of the cliffs and smiled. He indicated with his finger where his villa sat.

Gwen followed his finger in dismay. "That is your home? Do we have to climb?"

He smiled and looked at the Duchess.

"No, there is a path for us to ride up if you wish. It will not take long for you to grow accustomed to the terrain, or the year-long summer. In England the weather does not encourage you to be outdoors much. In *Italia*, you do not want to be indoors much."

"It sounds heavenly."

"And now we *arrivare. Benvenuti in Italia.*"

HENRIETTA, Dowager Duchess of Loring, was nervous. She, who had held together a dukedom for decades and had rubbed noses with royalty, was shaking. During her courtship with Luca, she had never met his son, Giovanni, who had been away at school at the time. Why did it matter to her what he thought of her? She knew it should not, but knowing how hurt Luca still was, she was afraid Giovanni would hold it against her. Would he resent his father bringing her here unannounced? True, Luca was still the Count, but it sounded as if he had handed over the reins to his son.

They rode on donkeys up the steep, white rocky path to the villa. Fragrant flowers with brilliant red and pink blooms lined the garden walls, seemingly growing from their stones, and pervaded her senses, sending her back in time again. At the top, they entered through iron gates to a terrace that floated above the earth; the clouds seemed to rotate around this very spot. It was as close to heaven as she could imagine.

She dismounted with Luca's help, and he led her across the stone-

walled terrace which overlooked the sea as the sun continued its descent.

"This was always your favourite time of day."

"Yes it was. I love it now as much as I did then."

They stood there watching until the sun fell beyond the horizon. The rest of the world faded from their view. When they turned, there were no more servants or family about.

"Everyone must have given up on us."

"I think they chose to give us time, for which I am grateful."

They searched each other's eyes.

"I don't know if I can do this, Luca."

"Don't think right now." He bent his head and placed a gentle kiss on her lips.

She had to stop herself from gasping out loud.

"Shall we go in to dinner? I am ready to eat a decent meal. Maybe you will be fortunate and they will have *lasagne*."

"You remember my favourite dish," she said, surprised.

"*Si.* I remember everything."

He led her through the front door and towards the dining room, where they could hear sounds of laughter and companionship.

"It sounds like our families are feeling agreeable thus far."

"Andrew gets along with everyone."

"He is not certain what to think of me."

"I am not certain what to think of you."

Luca laughed. "I admire him for wanting to protect you."

"Yes, but I need not be his concern."

"A good man will always have concern for those he loves."

They stood before the door to the dining room. "You are trembling."

"I am nervous."

"That is very unlike you."

"I know." For some reason, she felt there was more at stake this time.

"My son, he will love you."

"Will he?"

"Of course. If you make me happy, he is happy. The same with your grandson."

Henrietta was not so confident that would be the case, but she followed him to the dining room. The men stood as they entered. Giovanni was the picture of Luca, with the exception of his eyes. She would have known he was Luca's son anywhere.

Giovanni made eye contact with her, and for a moment she was not sure he would welcome her. But then he smiled and walked toward her with his arms out. He took her hands and kissed them, and then each cheek, as he would family.

"At last I meet *la Duchessa*, he said in broken English. "Forgive me. I do not have many opportunity to speak the English. *Benvenuta nella nostra casa.*"

"*Grazie*, Giovanni. It is a pleasure to meet you at last."

"Please join us." He indicated the table. His wife Rosa was introduced.

Henrietta was seated at the place of honour opposite Luca.

"Forgive us for not waiting. You seemed *preoccupata.*" Rosa smiled.

The Italians were much more open about their emotions and feelings. Henrietta was still not comfortable with that. She didn't know how she felt. "I am glad you did not wait. We did not realize how long we were out on the terrace."

The younger couples looked at each other and smiled. Henrietta had difficulty not blushing and squirming in her seat.

"The sunsets here have no comparison," Luca said. "It is easy to be lost in their beauty." He stared at Henrietta over his glass as he took a sip of wine. She looked down at her plate. At one time she had been used to flirtation. She had been a wealthy duchess, and many men had sought her attention. She was not the same person anymore. Was it worth throwing her heart open again? She felt young once more; she wanted to enjoy her time, however short it was. She now knew how precious each moment was.

"Gran?" She heard Andrew interrupt her contemplations.

"Forgive me. Being here has brought back so many memories."

"Good ones, I hope," Giovanni said.

"Yes," and "mostly," she added quietly.

"Tell us about your courtship," Rosa said boldly.

"I am not certain that is wise," the Dowager said.

"Curious minds wish to know." Andrew smiled devilishly.

"It was a beautiful experience," the Conte said. "Your grandmother had just come out of mourning and accompanied her son, the new duke, on a holiday."

"Yes, Robert was not doing well with his father's loss and the heavy burden of his new responsibilities. I thought touring the Continent would divert him and help him relax. We were in Paris and attending a ball. I forget whose ball." She waved her hand. "There were many English in France in those days."

"I remember the first time I saw her. There was no other woman in the room when she was present. Not only for me, but for all the gentleman. She was also a great beauty then."

Henrietta again found herself fighting a flush. She waved her hand again dismissively to make light of Luca's comment.

"I still remember the gown of deep blue Henrietta was wearing. Her hair was high on her head with her golden curls falling around. She wore a tiara with a large blue stone, and a matching necklace," he said as he stared off into the distance, imaging the scene.

"The Loring sapphires," Andrew stated.

Henrietta nodded. "I still have that gown to this day."

"I would love to see you in it again," Luca said.

"Then you best stop feeding me my favourite dishes." She winked and took another bite of the heavenly dessert they called *bavarese lombarda*.

"What happened after that?" Gwen asked, not satisfied with hearing only the partial story.

"I hurried across the dance floor to be the first to solicit Henrietta's hand," the Conte said.

"And were you the first?"

"No." He shook his head. "I had to wait several dances before I could obtain an introduction. I circled the dance floor waiting for my moment. A hunter stalking his prey." He laughed.

Henrietta shivered unconsciously. She remembered feeling watched that evening. It was a seductive feeling—wondering who by and whether they would be welcome if she ever discovered who they were.

"Do you remember meeting the Conte so vividly?" Gwen asked the Dowager.

"I do. I remember he cut in front of my next partner," the Dowager said saucily.

Andrew laughed. "And what did you have to say to that?"

"She told me I had better be worth her time," Luca answered.

Everyone laughed. "I can hear Gran saying the words," Andrew said.

"It was worth it. The dance was magical," she assured everyone at the table.

"It certainly was. The crowd parted and watched us dance the new waltz," Luca said reminiscing.

"I did not realize they had done so until the dance was over."

"Yes. It was only you and me when we danced."

"I imagine it was rather scandalous in those days," Gwen said.

"I never minded shocking people, dear. It was Paris, after all," Henrietta remarked with a gleam in her eye.

"What happened after that? Rosa asked.

"I never had another partner." The Dowager laughed.

"No one else would dance with you?" Rosa was astonished.

"No, dear. I only danced with Luca the rest of the evening."

"I do not share well," he explained.

Gwen and Rosa sighed.

"Perhaps we should retire to the *terrazza* and enjoy a little dancing by moonlight tonight."

"I've never danced in the moonlight," Gwen said.

"Then we must!" the Conte exclaimed. "It is a tradition here."

He sent for musicians, and the party returned outdoors to the beautiful stone terrace, with the sea to one side and a beautiful garden to the other. A brilliant full moon lit the way. It felt magical, and

Henrietta did not intend to think about, nor act, her age this night, as Luca took her into his arms.

A harp and violin began to strum the waltz they had danced to so long ago. Once again she was lost to the world around her, but as she sailed around the terrace in Luca's arms, she wasn't sure she would be able to let go this time.

CHAPTER 3

ndrew watched the scene before him with astonishment. His grandmother was acting as if she was well, not a grand-mother, he pondered, as she was twirled around in the Conte's arms.

"What is the matter, Andrew?" Gwen asked as she danced with him. His eyes were still following the Dowager and the Conte.

"Do you think she is disguised? Just look at them," he insisted.

"They look like two people enjoying themselves immensely," she said approvingly.

"But…she is acting like a ninny!" he protested.

"She is not. We are not in a society ballroom, Andrew. I think it is nice to see her let her hair down and enjoy herself."

"I suppose," he said doubtfully.

"Why shouldn't she have fun and fall in love?" Gwen reasoned.

"She is my grandmother. It is not done." He thought a moment. "At least, not by her. She would be making a jest of anyone else acting as such in England."

"We are not in England."

"No. We're not."

"When in Rome…"

"You could not resist, could you?"

She smiled brilliantly up at him. He bent his head down and kissed her.

"Not here, Andrew!"

"I could not resist," he smiled rakishly.

"Perhaps we should retire for the night," she suggested.

"I would be happy to, if these two love birds would cease their display."

"Let her have fun. Have you ever seen her so happy?"

"No, and it is acutely uncomfortable, I might point out."

"It is none of your business, I might point out."

"Indeed it is. She made my love-life her business."

"Which turned out splendidly for you, did it not? But, still, you had a choice."

"I would like to think we would have found each other without her help."

"She would never have forced either of us to do anything."

"No, but if she hadn't approved, she would have found a way to separate us."

"I think we should give it time and see what happens. She has lived her proper life; she deserves to live however she sees fit now."

"I am going to speak to her." Andrew made to go and talk to her at that moment, but Gwen stopped him gently with her hand.

"This is not the time. Let us retire. She can take care of herself. I promise."

"Very well. I will wait—for now," he said and reluctantly followed his wife to their room.

"Luca, dawn is breaking."

"Mmhmm." He continued to whirl her about, even though they had sent the musicians to bed long ago, when the younger ones had retired.

"As much as I adore dancing with you, you will soon be holding the both of us upright."

"Very well, *mia bella*, but I want to dance with you again."

"I've no objection, but I do need more rest these days if I am to dance the night away."

He led her gently into the house to her chamber. He kissed her goodbye at the door. "Until we meet again."

"Sweet dreams, Luca."

She entered her room and was shocked to find Andrew fully clothed, minus his cravat, asleep on a chair. She debated falling into her bed and letting him wake later, but that would ultimately disturb her sleep. She closed the door with a click and cleared her throat. He stirred, then realized where he was and his purpose. He opened an eye. "It rather lessens the effect when you fall asleep doesn't it?" he said sheepishly with a smile.

"If you mean that you were waiting for me in order to reprimand me about my behaviour, then yes. I've no intention of listening to you now. You may try again at a later time if you like." She set her jewellery on the dressing table and began to remove the pins from her hair. She had dismissed Hanson for the night hours ago.

"You don't want to hear what I have to say, do you?"

"Not particularly," she said with a yawn. "However, you are my grandson, and I know you mean well, so I will pretend to be attentive."

He sighed.

"Yes, yes. I am old and am acting like a fool." She put words in his mouth.

"That was not precisely how I would have phrased it," he said defensively.

"That is how I would have heard it."

"You know I only want to protect you."

"I do, and as an expert meddler, I've learned when to back away."

"And this is one of those times."

"Indeed. And now, unless you wish to see more of your old gran than you or I intended, you best go back to your room."

"No need for threats." He held up his hands and kissed her on the cheek. "Sleep well, Gran."

"Sleep well, dear."

~

WHEN HENRIETTA WAS FINALLY able to pull herself out of bed around noon and make her way downstairs, the only person around when she entered the breakfast room was Giovanni.

"*Buongiorno, Giovanni,*" she greeted him.

"*Buongiorno, Duchessa,*" he replied.

"Has everyone gone out?"

"*Si,* my father, he shows the Abbotts some vistas for painting, and Rosa has gone into the village to prepare for the *festa.*" He rang for someone to come and serve her.

"I should have asked that they wake me."

"Father insisted they let you sleep."

"He is very good." A maid set a tray of chocolate and rolls before her. Luca must have asked for her favourites to be prepared yet again. She smiled.

"*Si.* He would do anything for you."

"I know. He is a wonderful man." She sipped her drink thoughtfully.

"I am pleased to see him so happy again," Giovanni said after a bit of hesitation.

She looked up to his enquiring stare.

"But you think I will hurt him all over again," she said frankly.

"I worry that he will not be well this time if you leave once more," he admitted.

"I have made him no promises, as I did before."

"*Comprendo.* I only ask that you not make him believe there is the chance...that you not stay long and break his heart again." Giovanni gestured with his hands as if to make her understand that he was afraid he wasn't making himself understood.

"I never intended to the first time," she said quietly.

"May I ask what happened? My father never tells me this."

"My son was having difficulties as the new duke, and also with my relationship with your father. My daughter was about to make her debut in London." She paused a moment, trying to choose her words wisely. "I felt my children needed me more at that time."

"More than taking your own happiness?" he asked with surprise.

She looked away so he would not see her fight back tears. "Yes."

"Did your children know you had promised to wed my father?"

"No. I did not tell them, even though Robert was travelling with me. He was angry about our relationship. It became apparent that he would need much guidance before he was able to assume his father's place."

"I understand, but it still saddens me. It seems there should have been a way." Giovanni looked away.

"Love should conquer all?" Henrietta offered.

"*Si*," he said, turning to search her face.

"Sometimes, dear, it is not so simple. I could have chosen Luca over my children, but there would have been many difficulties for them. I had always thought I would be able to return to him, but by the time Robert was capable of handling matters on his own, Elizabeth had become ill and eventually she died. I felt her children needed me."

"For thirty years?" Giovanni questioned in disbelief.

"I had no way of knowing Luca had not moved on. At a certain point, my dear, one ceases to put one's self first."

"I am a father. I do understand this."

"And one day you wake up and find you are old, without knowing how it happened."

"I do not call you old, but *saggia* or *intelligente*," he corrected, choosing words she might understand. "No one knows how much time they have left. Why not enjoy it day by day?"

"I never said I had not enjoyed myself. But I see your meaning. I will do my best to not hurt him, Giovanni."

"*Grazie*. It is all I can ask." He bowed and left the room, leaving her feeling thoughtful and restless. She decided to take a walk and try to clear her mind.

She meandered through the garden towards the orchards. She

expected it would be easier to have some time alone there. She needed to think about what Giovanni had said—about the implications of her behaviour and Luca's. Frankly, everything had happened so fast she had not thought much beyond the present. She needed to separate herself from this intoxicating paradise. It was hard to remember herself in Luca's presence.

She found a bench in the orchard on a steep slope, where it looked as if she would roll into the sea if she leaned forward. She looked up to the sky for answers and watched the clouds swirl overhead as the breeze tousled her hair about.

When she wasn't with Luca, she did have doubts. More likely, rational thought pervaded when she was alone. Perhaps Giovanni was right. She should leave now. She still loved Luca, but she did not know if she could stay. She had been alone too long to start over. She was set in her ways, she didn't mind her own company and she was content by herself. But she liked the way she felt when she was with him. She was the centre of someone's attention again. She had never been neglected, but it was different when you were someone's focus instead of a peripheral party.

"What are you thinking, *mia bella?*" Luca asked quietly from behind her.

She did not answer for a time as she contemplated her answer. She was never one to dance around the truth. "About the future," she replied at last.

"Am I in this future you think of?"

"It would be impertinent for me to assume such a thing, Luca," she said with her usual *sangfroid.*

"Please tell me you have not reformed yourself so much that you are not impertinent."

"Oh, rest assured I am not reformed. Reformation is highly overrated."

"Indeed," he said.

"The truth is, I do not know what the future holds. I was trying to envision what it would look like if we were together or apart. It is difficult to see myself beginning again at this point in my life."

"And if I came to England with you?"

She turned to look at him. "You would do that?"

"If it meant waking up by your side every morning, *si*. I love *Italia*, but not so much as I love you. It has never been the same without you."

"Luca," she whispered, uncomfortable with his Italian sentimentality. She had never been one to dwell on what-ifs, but he made her feel regret.

"Etta," he replied.

"Please do not ask anything of me yet, Luca."

He sighed and looked away. "Is it your grandson?"

"No, it is not Andrew, although I would prefer to have his blessing."

"Why must we have everyone's permission?" Luca held his hands out wide with exasperation. "We are the heads of our families, yet we seek to please them? Is it not time for our happiness?"

She turned back and watched the sea, pondering this question.

"The seas, the winds, the mountains, they are timeless. But we are not. We are nearer that age when our bodies and minds begin to fail," she reasoned.

"So we do it together. But at least we are together."

"I'm afraid for that, Luca. I never envisioned us spooning one another our meals."

"Do you think I will love you less with more silver hair or one more wrinkle?"

"Whatever do you mean, one more?" She feigned shock, although she would never get used to looking like a shrivelled prune when that day came.

"Will you walk with me?" he asked. "Enjoy one day at a time and see where that leads us?"

"If you think you can accept my decision in the end," she said candidly.

"What choice will I have?"

"I do not wish to leave as I did before. There may never be another chance."

"Very well. I agree to accept your decision."

"Then let us enjoy the day. I believe I would fancy a walk through the orchard."

"And a glass of our *limonata speciale* when we are finished?"

"Of course. Why else would I bother to exert myself if not with an ulterior motive? I even promise to dance with you tonight for *cannoli*."

"I am most happy to know you have not changed, Etta." He pulled her close and kissed the top of her head.

"Oh, many things have changed, but fortunately my wits are still tactless."

THEY WALKED for some time through the lemon, lime, and olive trees, reminiscing and catching up on the goings-on in each other's lives over decades past. They found themselves hand-in-hand as if scarcely a day had passed. It was comfortable.

"Do you care to walk to the beach? I think I would like to feel sand and water on my feet before I die," she pronounced.

"You think you are to die soon?" he asked with humour written on his face.

"Who can ever tell? Walking all the way down there, it might be the last thing I do," she said as she warily eyed the steep path downwards.

"I shall carry you then."

"Then we shall both die," she retorted.

"You think me so feeble, I must now prove my manliness," he said as he scooped her up effortlessly.

"This is most unnecessary, Luca," she said, though her protest ended and she enjoyed being in his arms. When they arrived at the beach he still had not set her down. "Do you mean to toss me in the water?"

He smiled. "The thought had occurred to me. It would not be too cold to rescue you here."

"Do I appear to be a damsel in distress?"

He subtly turned and looked back up the steep path he had just carried her down, but said not a word.

"You may set me down now."

"I was looking for a place to release you. You will need to remove your slippers."

"I suppose I will."

"However, I see no place but the sand, and you will not want to ruin your dress. Therefore, I am concluding that I must remove your slippers before I put you down."

"I..." He had already begun to do so before she could object. "*Grazie*."

He gently placed her on the sand, which felt wet and gritty, even through her stockings. She dared not ask Luca to remove those, nor display her hind end in the air to do so herself.

"What do you think of the Italian sand?" he asked as he removed his own boots and stockings. She looked away.

"It is much different than the pebbled beaches in England. It feels strange, like I am sinking."

"You are."

She looked down, and her feet did, in fact, appear to be sinking into the sand. She grabbed onto Luca's arm. "Is it quicksand?"

"No, you won't go far."

"How very reassuring."

"Let us walk to the water."

She continued to hold onto him with one arm, as she was not too certain about this sinking sand. She lifted her skirts with the other hand and walked to the edge of the sea. As a gentle wave came over their feet, she laughed.

"Do you like it?"

"I believe I do. I expected it to be cold like the sea in England, but it feels like bath water."

"I told you so."

"I know. I have thought about it many times over the years and wished I had tried it. But, now I know at last. I think it is good I did not know, or it would have made my decision to leave harder."

"I hope you will consider it this time in your decision."

"Do you always know what you want so clearly?"

"Almost always. And I usually get what I want."

"Are you certain now that you do not want me because you lost me before?" she asked candidly.

"*Si*. I want you the same now as then. I want to be more than your *cisibeo, mia bella*."

"It has been many years since I had any such thing. You are hardly the type."

"*Grazie*," he laughed. She had once had a large following of tulips who made fools of themselves over her.

As they were standing there laughing, a large wave caught them by surprise and soaked her skirts.

'Oh!" she exclaimed breathlessly as she was surprised by the water spraying her lower half.

"Refreshing is it not? You should try to swim," he said as he playfully fell back into the water. He stood back up and lifted his shirt to wring it out. She tried not to stare.

"No, I thank you. I think my dignity has had enough tarnishing for one day."

"If this is tarnished, I like it very much," he said as he tucked a loose silver strand of hair back behind her ear. He kissed her on top of the head, and then turned her around. She was surprised but unafraid in his arms. He continued to take her through some steps of a dance, ending up with a dip backwards. For a moment, she thought he would truly drop her in the water, but he was either funning or had changed his mind, for he began to lead her back out of the sea. She shook her skirts out as he gathered their shoes from the beach. She eyed them, and then looked down at her sand-covered feet.

"How do we manage the shoes?"

"Ah, this is the most difficult part. You must choose between sand and being wet."

"Must I?" she asked with wide eyes.

He chuckled. "No, I suppose I must." He put his boots on over his sandy feet and scooped her up again while she was still pondering her choices.

"It is not necessary to carry me up the hill. For all I appreciate the pampering, I am not decrepit."

"I know this, but how else am I to have you in my arms all day? Besides, I promised you I would not make you climb."

She cast him a look, to which he smiled rakishly. "You are about to make me think I am too old for you, Luca."

"Age is a state of mind, *mia bella*."

"I agree to some extent, I am the first to enjoy myself, but everything is not as it was thirty-four years ago."

"You should not worry so much."

"I did not worry until you looked at me in such a way." Then she had to concern herself with thoughts she hadn't had in ages. He looked at her in that way once again and her heart began to race.

"The boys will be thinking we have been up to mischief if they see us like this." He laughed and raised a mocking, scandalized eyebrow.

"Let them think what they like." She thrust out her chin.

"Easy for you to say. I must make a good impression on your grandson."

It was her turn to laugh. "This should be diverting. Whoever would have thought we would be trying to impress each other's children and grandchildren at our age?"

"Ah, but we do it for the right reasons."

As they made it back to the top of the path, they saw Andrew and Gwen walking hand in hand the other direction.

"Should we hide?"

"Hiding is undignified."

"So is explaining our appearance to your grandchildren."

"We have done nothing to be ashamed of, Luca."

He gave her a look.

"Oh, very well, let us wait until they pass."

"Over here," he whispered in her ear. He led her to a trellis covered in vines, where they waited until Andrew and Gwen had moved out of sight.

"That was close."

"I do not know why you are worried so much. He will come around."

"You said you wanted his blessing?" he said, exasperated.

"He will be more suspicious if he thinks we are sneaking around. I cannot explain, but trust me, be yourself."

"Fickle is the English word I am looking for, I think," he said with his handsome half-grin.

"Yes, that words suits," she said with a wink. "I think I will go and change now. Thank you for the lovely time."

"No, thank you, my dearest." He kissed her hand and watched her walk away with the grace of a duchess.

ANDREW AND GWEN hurried in the other direction when they saw the Conte and his grandmother coming up the path looking wet and tousled. Gwen was mostly trying to stop Andrew from going to enquire about their behaviour.

"It is not your place to ask," she scolded before he could say anything.

"It is so unlike her," he said in confusion. "Have you ever before seen her with a hair out of place? Let alone soaking wet and covered in sand?" He covered his eyes to erase the image.

"I am certain it is not what you think."

"I do not know what to think. Is he sneaking a powder into her drink? Or is she infatuated?"

"Andrew," Gwen chided softly.

"I do want her to be happy," he added as if trying to convince himself.

"As do I. She seems smitten with him."

"Did we act in such a fashion? I believe I heard that term to describe us once or twice."

She nodded.

"Surely not," he said with disgust. "In front of people?"

She nodded again with a grin.

"I wonder if she has been pining for him all these years without a word? If this is her true self?" he contemplated.

"I was not under the impression she was leading a miserable existence. She makes the best of her situation."

"Yes, I suppose so. She is not one to pine."

"Do you think she means to stay here when we leave for Christmas?" Gwen asked.

"Who can say? I think my gran has another side to her that I have never seen. I suppose I need to come to terms with it, or then she will be unhappy because I am unhappy."

"I *think* I follow your logic, but I understand your meaning. I think it wise to be supportive, but only offer advice if it is asked for."

"I will do my best. It will require frequent reminders. And kisses. Loads of kisses to keep me distracted."

"I will do my best to oblige."

CHAPTER 4

While Gwen and Andrew were preoccupied in a small grotto, a loud horn sounded.

"What was that?" Gwen raised her head to ask.

"It sounded like a horn," Andrew replied helpfully.

"I know that, but where is it coming from? The beach?"

"Very likely," he replied while continuing to shower his love with attention.

"Do you think someone is in trouble?" she persisted.

He sighed, realising Gwen was distracted beyond redemption. "Very likely. I will go and look."

He rose and walked over to the edge of the cliff, and saw that a fishing vessel appeared to be capsized and the villagers were running to help at the call of the horn.

"Run to the house for help! A boat has capsized!" he shouted as he took off running toward the path down to the beach.

Gwen obeyed, yelling for him to be careful as she did.

By the time Andrew made it to the shore, Luca and Giovanni were already there. Giovanni was hurriedly rowing a small boat filled with men to pick up those they could find, and Luca was organising more men along a line of rope trailing behind the boat. Andrew had heard of such rescue efforts, but had never before been part of one.

"What can I do to help?"

Luca looked up momentarily with surprise to see Andrew there, but was grateful for the assistance.

"Use the spy-glass. Look for survivors."

Andrew nodded, momentarily relieved he would not have to try his hand at swimming in the sea. He had many times looked through such a glass over the battlefield. Looking out to sea proved to be a more formidable task, with no point for orientation. At last he decided to start from the cliffs and work his way out. He spotted Giovanni gathering survivors who clung along the rope—those who were able to hold on—and taking others into the rowing boat who could not. He spotted the overturned fishing vessel, and could see nothing of any more men.

"See anything?" Luca enquired once the fishermen were gathered and the rope was being pulled to the shore.

"Nothing but the fishing boat and those who are already retrieved. I would be happy for you to check for me though."

Luca ran over to count those who had been found and began a discourse with the men as they arrived on shore. There were villagers there to receive them and provide aid. As Giovanni rowed back in, some of the survivors began pleading to take the boat back out. One of the fisherman who could barely stand began arguing in violent Italian.

"Have we missed someone?" Andrew began searching the seas again worriedly at the man's obvious distress.

"No. They want to retrieve their catch. It was such a large haul, it was the reason for the boat turning over."

"They believe they can retrieve it?" Andrew asked in disbelief, thinking that there had been someone left out there drowning.

"They wish to try. It will feed many hungry mouths and provide for many months."

"They are exhausted. It will be impossible."

"Perhaps, but they feel they must try."

Andrew watched the men pleading, much like he had seen men begging for food when rations had been low on the Peninsula. He remembered the desperation when they had not known when they would eat again.

"It means that much to them?"

"*Si*." Luca nodded.

"Then let us help. We are fresh."

Andrew and Luca made their way to the rowing boat and spoke with Giovanni, who looked beaten from the efforts of rescuing twenty men. His father bade him wait on the shore while he and Andrew went in search of the fishing nets.

"Send more boats and more men. We will need more strength."

Giovanni nodded and went to seek more help, while Andrew tentatively climbed into the rowboat. He had sailed across the small lake on the estate as a boy with his cousins, but nothing compared to rowing against the waves on the ocean. By the time they reached the overturned fishing vessel, he had little energy left for searching for a few nets full of fish. He felt the errand to be fruitless. But it meant a livelihood to the villagers, so he vowed to try since they were in no fit state to do so themselves.

"So what do we do now?" Andrew asked Luca, who did not seem as fatigued as he felt, he noticed appreciatively.

Luca eyed him sceptically and said, "You would take orders from an old man you do not like?"

"I am a soldier," Andrew replied humorously. "I take orders well."

Luca chuckled. "*Touché*. First, we survey the boat."

"*Reconnoitre*. I know how to do that." Andrew nodded with admiration of the man's grasp of the English and French languages.

As they rowed slowly around the overturned vessel, Luca was deep in concentration, as if memorising every inch. Andrew was not sure what he was looking for. He looked down, trying to see through the water, but it was deep enough that he could not see as clearly as he'd been able to near the shore. He did not see any fish, as he had suspected. Luca began removing his boots and his shirt, revealing an impressively fit physique.

"I suppose, next, we go under the boat?" Andrew asked, not wanting to hear the answer.

"No," Luca replied. "*I* go under the boat. You wait here."

"Would it not be more useful for me to be under there with you?"

"No." He shook his head. "You are afraid. I don't have the energy to rescue you too, or explain to your grandmother."

"I was afraid at every battle, but I still did what needed to be done."

"You are here to save me if I need to be. You can help me row back."

Before Andrew could protest, Luca dived into the sea and disappeared under the boat. Andrew saw no sign of him for several minutes. Cursing, he finally began removing his own boots and shirt to search for the Conte, contemplating what he would tell his gran when he returned without her love. He had to admit: he liked Luca. The Conte had humour and self-assurance, not to mention that he was honourable, risking his life to provide for his people. He was a perfect match for Andrew's spirited grandmother. She would certainly give him a run for his money.

Andrew stood up and wobbled. He caught his balance and was grabbing his nose to jump in when Luca's head burst out of the water. Luca held onto the boat, and he took several deep breaths. He then began laughing.

"What is so deuced funny?" Andrew demanded.

"You should see the picture you make."

"I never pretended to be a sailor."

"No." Luca shook his head and fought to control his laughter.

"Did you find anything?" Andrew asked, trying not to laugh himself.

Luca smiled and struggled to hold up the end of a net. "*Si.* We will need many boats to bring this in."

"Why do they not use many small nets?"

"They do not hold as much."

Andrew stifled his ungentlemanly reply while still appreciative of Luca's humour.

"Do they return yet?" Luca asked.

Andrew looked toward the shore. "I see some boats coming."

"I pray there are enough." Luca held up the end of the net to Andrew again. "Hold this and do not let go. I must go for the other side. It is still tied to the fishing boat."

Andrew took hold of the massive ropes that made up the net. It was all he could do to maintain himself upright in the rowing boat as the fish caught within the net fought and struggled to free themselves from their prison. There had to be hundreds of them.

Giovanni rowed in with two other boats. "Where is my father?"

"He is loosening the other end."

Giovanni nodded and held his hands out for the ropes. *"Buon Dio!"* he exclaimed.

"I'm glad you brought several boats."

"The men warned me, but I had no idea it could be this much."

The men in the boats neared and then worked to tie the ropes between their craft. Luca emerged from the sea once more looking more tired this time. "He is human after all," Andrew chuckled to himself. "I was beginning to worry again."

"This end would not come loose. I had to stop for air a few times."

"And here I was admiring your ability to stay under so long."

"There is air under the fishing boat," Luca laughed. "I should have let you think me Neptune."

Another rowboat edged beside theirs and its crew helped to tie the end of the net between their vessel and Andrew's. Andrew hauled a tired Luca back in.

When the net was as secure as they could make it, Giovanni gave instructions in Italian. The assisting men crossed themselves and began to shout in unison something similar to the *heave-ho* the English sailors used. He caught the rhythm quickly, though every pull was a struggle. He thought to himself with every thrust of the oar that marriage must be making him soft. He dared not look towards the shore, for he knew it was far. He heard Luca working hard behind him, and that motivated him to continue pushing though every muscle in his body was burning with fire.

As they came closer to the shore, men waded out to meet them and help pull the catch in. Andrew had never been so happy to be out of a boat. A sentiment he had felt before, but he meant it this time. The grateful fisherman had the net of fish under control, so he and Luca stumbled onto the beach to rest.

Andrew fell face first into the sand, and Luca sat with his head and arms resting on his knees. Giovanni joined them, and the trio lay down in silence pondering the event, but mostly thankful it was over.

"Signor Abbott, please accept my gratitude. This is not your village or your people, so it was not your *responsabilità*, I think is the word," Giovanni looked at Andrew who nodded. "But we very much appreciate your help."

"Helping those in need is everyone's responsibility," he replied.

"*Grazie.*" The men shook hands.

"Besides, families help each other."

Luca's head popped up after hearing the exchange. He and Andrew looked meaningfully at each other and smiled.

After the fisherman had hauled the catch ashore and divided the booty, they began dispersing to their homes with plans to return with the slight evening tide to salvage the fishing vessel if possible. Luca, Giovanni and Andrew stood in order to make their way back home, looking at the steep cliff with trepidation.

"I do not look forward to this climb, but at least we do not have a load to carry," Luca remarked.

"All I think of is food," Giovanni said.

"I'm too tired and sore to eat, I think," Andrew reflected.

"Wait until the 'morrow. It will be worse," Luca warned.

"Yes, I remember from battle. The day after is always more painful."

"You must swim tomorrow. It will help the pains."

"Is there something I could do not involving water?" Andrew asked inquisitively.

"*Si.* We put you to work with the harvest," Giovanni teased.

"Perhaps it's time to go..." he jested with a friendly pat on Giovanni's back.

Luca's face fell, as if Andrew had touched a nerve.

"I speak in jest," Andrew reassured Luca.

"This time, I know. But soon you will go, and I fear she will go too."

"I cannot say what she will do, sir. I have never seen her this happy. But the choice is hers."

Luca nodded as they reached the villa, and Andrew and Giovanni rushed toward their wives, who were waiting anxiously for their return.

LUCA TRIED NOT to be disappointed that Henrietta was not there awaiting his arrival. Instead of going into the house to bathe for dinner, he wandered about the gardens deep in thought. Perhaps he needed to scale back his affections. Henrietta was not a woman who liked to feel smothered or be ordered about. If he could only make her see how good they were for one another, to see things as he saw them...he had to find a way. She seemed to still love him, but she never put herself first. When she was younger, she would not have minded leaving England. But now? Most people his age were settled in one place and afraid of change. Perhaps she was not certain what she wanted to do with herself now either since she was travelling. His soul had not found rest without her. Never a day went by that he did not think of her and pray that God would help them find their way together again. He did not believe they had been reunited by coincidence, but he also did not want to ruin his last chance. He looked up to see the Duchess standing there looking vexed.

"How dare you scare me like that? You speak your fancy words of growing old together, then I find you have gone out to rescue fisherman as if you were two-and-twenty!"

"Ah, so you do care," he said with an amused expression.

"I wish I did not." She crossed her arms.

"I am fine, as are all the fisherman, thank you. We even managed to save the catch."

"You went out there for fish?" She moved her hands to her hips.

"It meant a great deal to the villagers," he explained calmly.

"There are plenty more fish in the sea!"

"Not a fact I wish to be reminded of at this time," he muttered.

"Why do you not fight like most Italians? Instead, you smile and speak calmly."

"I wish to save my passions for other things." He smiled once more.

She blushed. "You will not be let off so easily," she protested. "I am too old for you to give me frights like this!"

"As you can see I am fine. There was never any danger. To me, at least."

She eyed him, wishing to convey her anxieties to him, but she could not stay cross with him.

"Forgive me?" he pleaded as he took her hands in his and brought them to his lips with a gentle kiss. "I have only just found you again. Do you think me so foolish as to throw it all away over fish?"

"But I was told..."

"Shh. I don't want to argue." He hushed her with his fingertips and drew her in for another kiss.

AFTER THE MEN had cleaned and dressed for dinner, they met the ladies in the *salotto*. The men were extremely tired, but did their best to be pleasant dinner companions. Rosa had been very busy organising the festival to celebrate the harvesting of the grapes.

Giovanni asked, "Is everything ready for the *festa*? We begin the gathering and treading tomorrow."

"*Si*. All we need is the grapes." She smiled.

"I have never attended a *festa dell' uva*. I assume it has something to do with wine?" Andrew asked.

"*Si*. We bless the harvest, and celebrate God's blessing on us." Rosa answered.

"And have a little fun." Luca added with a wink.

"That sounds lovely," Gwen replied.

"You may help me in the village tomorrow, if you like," Rosa invited.

"Yes, thank you. I would like to pick up some more paints as well."

"When will we see your paintings?"

"I shall have one ready soon. It is a surprise." Gwen looked toward Andrew. "Will you help with the grape harvest?

Andrew laughed. "I am not certain they will welcome my assistance after today."

"There will be no swimming or rowing involved in picking grapes," Luca teased.

"Am I to deduce you were the one who was in danger today?" the Dowager asked.

"Not at all," Luca interceded.

"Only in danger of losing my manliness," Andrew laughed. "I am not cut out to be a sailor."

"No, I could have told you as much." Gwen chimed in.

"Thank you for the support, dear," he said with a hint of sarcasm.

"But you are good at many other things," she added.

"Stop now, please!" Andrew pleaded with his hands.

"But you did run the plantation," she pointed out. "So you should be better at the harvest."

"He actually did very well today," Luca said. "I would have him help me anytime."

"*Si.* We would not have been able to bring the catch in without him," Giovanni said gratefully.

"And that will feed the villagers for a long time."

"And I have not had such a good laugh in a long time either," Luca added.

"Laughs I can tolerate." Andrew agreed.

CHAPTER 5

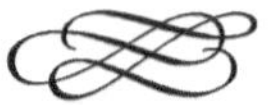

osa and Gwen rode in a cart down to the village. They waved towards the men who were cutting the grapes from the vines and placing them into large carts.

"This is an important festival for your village?" Gwen asked Rosa.

"*Si*. It is only once a year. We have other crops of course, but this is the largest."

"Is there much left to do for preparations?"

"No, we only hang the garland and flowers. Everything else is ready. The keeper of the fountain will change the water to wine in the morning. The village ladies will put out the food on the tables tomorrow as well."

Rosa pulled into the village and parked the cart at the inn. Gwen noticed people stare, even though she had pinned her red hair under her bonnet. Rosa noticed too, and simply smiled and waved at them to remind them Gwen was her guest.

"I apologise. They are not used to seeing foreigners."

"I am used to it. I doubt I'll ever be comfortable with it. People stare at my hair at home too."

"You have great beauty. Even more because you are humble." Rosa added kindly.

"Thank you, Rosa," Gwen said timidly.

"So we buy your paints first? Many shops will close early to prepare for tomorrow."

"Thank you, yes. I would like to finish my painting before we leave."

"Ah, *si*. Your surprise. Will you give me a hint?"

Gwen smiled. "It is a gift for the Conte."

"La Duchessa?"

Gwen nodded.

Rosa's face fell a bit.

"Is something wrong, Rosa?"

"Do you think she will leave him again?"

"Oh, I hope not!" Gwen's hands flew to her face. "Oh, dear, she is so happy with him, I had not considered that."

"Luca tells Giovanni he does not think she will stay. Giovanni is very worried for his father. His heart was very broken last time. He still loves her very much."

"And she loves him. I can tell. I watch people—I suppose that comes with being an artist. But I have never seen two people more in love and so well suited. However, she is very stubborn and may not see what is best for her."

"Then we must help her see," Rosa said determinedly, becoming passionate and accentuating her words.

"But how?"

"I have an idea. I will speak to Giovanni, but you must finish the painting in time, *si*?"

"I think I can," Gwen said hesitantly.

"Then you take the cart back now. You send someone for me this afternoon."

"Very well. I hope this works."

"Me too." Rosa crossed herself with a look toward the heavens.

They purchased the paints, and Gwen headed off to finish her surprise.

~

THE MEN WORKING in the fields had taken a break for lunch. Andrew was wandering around enjoying the beauty of the Italian countryside, when he found his grandmother sitting on a bench looking soulful.

"Hello, Gran," he greeted. "May I join you?"

"Certainly." She patted the seat beside her.

"Had your fill of picking grapes already?" she teased.

"They are taking a break for the noonday meal."

"Is Gwen returned from the village yet?"

"Yes, but she is working on a painting she needs to finish today."

"Ah, yes. The surprise. I will go check on her in a while."

"You looked deep in thought when I found you. Care to talk about it?"

She sighed heavily. "I am sure it is obvious to you. You know me as well as anyone."

"The Conte?"

"I am having difficulty deciding what I should do."

"What is there to decide? You love each other and there is no reason you cannot be together now."

"I can think of several."

"Several that truly matter?"

She looked toward his face with scepticism and searched his eyes. "You have altered your opinion then."

He gave a slight shrug. "I have."

She gave a satisfied smile. "That is wise. He is a wonderful man. What made you change your mind?"

"There was no one thing. He has earned my respect during our stay. I never thought anyone would be good enough for you. But, alas, that is not for me to decide. If you are happy, I think him an excellent man. You will keep him on his toes."

She laughed in delight. "You wouldn't have to worry over me then, at least."

He looked at her with hurt. "You think you are a burden to me?"

"Not a burden, precisely, but you are starting your new life. You should not need to worry about your aged gran."

"I can't explain my feelings. I know ageing is hard, but having you be part of our lives is important to Gwen and me. I want to make sure you know you are wanted. You have always been there for me and I want to be there for you. Not because I owe anything to you, but because I want you to be a part of my life, and my children's lives."

"Are you certain it is not only so you may harass me and trade barbs?" she jested, though the tears were forming in her eyes.

"That is only a side benefit."

She harrumphed with pleasure.

"Whatever you decide, I will support you. I did not want to be a reason to hinder your future happiness." He reached his arm around her and placed a gentle kiss on her head.

"I know. Thank you. Now that is enough sentimentality from you for today. Go and pick grapes, and I will go check on your bride."

"As you wish," he said with a mischievous grin.

SOMETHING WASN'T QUITE RIGHT. It was always hard to paint a portrait from memory, but she could not ask the Duchess to pose or it would ruin the surprise. Gwen had managed most of the likeness quite well, but something about the Dowager's eyes wasn't right. She had not been able to capture the magical twinkle the Duchess had when she looked at the Conte. Frustrated, Gwen wiped the paint off of her brushes and was about to take a break. Sometimes, when one had looked at the same thing for too long, it all became a blur.

"There you are!"

Gwen jumped to cover the painting.

"Well, hello, Grandmother. I was just thinking about you. Do you need something?"

"Not particularly. Andrew said you were in a hurry to finish your painting, so I thought I would check on you."

"He is right. I am trying to finish. Would you care to sit with me while I paint? I only have one small part to do."

"I would be delighted, though I believe I will send for refreshments. I am feeling a trifle thirsty."

As the Dowager asked a servant for tea, Gwen thought there must have been a divine intervention. Now she only needed Luca to walk by, so the Dowager would look at him in that way of hers. Perhaps if Gwen encouraged her to talk more about him...

"Any more moonlit dancing with the handsome Conte?" she prodded.

As she expected, the Dowager gave her a look as if she were being impertinent, but her eyes were sparkling.

"Well?" Gwen laughed as she stroked and dabbed paints to capture the moment.

"Perhaps."

"Perhaps? That is all I am to know?"

"Very well. There have been walks through the orchard, splashing in the sea, dancing on the sand..."

"And..."

"And a stolen kiss or two."

Gwen was lost in the moment, thinking of her own stolen kisses, when she remembered her painting.

"He sounds like a dream come true." She finally broke the silence.

The Dowager was looking out over the terrace, lost in her own thoughts. Long enough for Gwen to finish, and for her to capture that look, just as she'd wanted. "I think I will go rest before dinner," the Dowager stated.

"I might do the same. I do not think there will be much time for rest tomorrow after hearing Rosa speak about it."

"Yes, the Italians know how to throw a party. I suspect there will be wonderful food and dancing until dawn."

"It is hard to believe a month has already passed since we arrived," Gwen remarked. "It is already almost time to leave for France."

The Dowager's face grew sombre at the reminder. Time had escaped her. If it was time to leave for France, then it was time to make a decision.

CHAPTER 6

A warm breeze from the water freshened the clear evening. The small village was decorated to enchant. Every white-stoned house and shop was adorned with brilliant baskets overflowing with red, purple and yellow flowers. Vines were hung from tiled roof to tiled roof, and the fountain at the centre of the square was flowing with wine.

Barrels were readied to receive their fruit of the vine and tables of foods were laid out as musicians began to strum tunes, signalling an evening of dancing to come. Children ran about in wild anticipation outside, while inside the final touches were made to costume and gown.

At the villa, the families were also in preparation for the festival. The men were relieved to have the harvest over with, and looking forward to relaxing. The women were anxious to see the party go without incident.

The Dowager was sitting in her apartment with butterflies in her stomach. The time had come to make a decision, and she was not yet ready to make a declaration—such a permanent one. She knew it was time for Andrew and Gwen to head for France for the Christmas season. Perhaps she could convince Luca to come to England again in the spring and see if their feelings had remained the same. She reasoned thus with herself, but could not feel comfortable with either choice. The knock came on her door, indicating it was time to leave.

She made her way out of her room feeling solemn, knowing she would likely be breaking Luca's heart yet again tonight. It was a feeling akin to walking to the gallows, she thought, except the pain would not end. She looked down at the blue dress she had found to wear for Luca and had to hold back tears. She took a deep breath and walked down the stairs. She would enjoy her last night with him and let come what may.

Luca was waiting for her when she arrived at the bottom step.

"*Mia bella, il mio amore.*" He took her hand a placed a tender kiss on it.

"*Grazie*," she replied, while feeling her heart breaking as she looked into his handsome face. She wanted to remember him like this forever.

"I think you are overdressed for this occasion, but we will make do." He chuckled as he led her to her ride.

"Nonsense. One can never be overdressed," she said, though she doubted her words as Luca hoisted her on to a donkey.

"If you say so, *mia bella.*"

The family paraded down the path from the villa, leading the carts of grapes. They were greeted with loud cheers from the villagers. When the caravan stopped, the Conte dismounted and assisted the Dowager to the murmurs of the crowd.

"*Benvenuti alla festa dell'uva!*" he greeted his people, to louds cheers. "I have with me honoured guests from *Inghilterra: la Duchessa* de Loring, and the Abbotts."

Whispers of awe followed the announcement of the Duchess, who looked the part, and shouts of praise greeted Andrew's introduction. Word had spread of the Englishman's help with the fishing boat's rescue.

"Now, let us begin!" he said with excitement.

The local priest stepped forward to bless the harvest, and then the workers began loading the grapes into the large barrels. As they worked, the Conte leaned over to the Dowager, "What do you think?"

"Are the villagers going to tread the grapes?"

"*Si*," he said with a smile.

"I believe my great-granddaughter, Amelia, did this in France."

"It is a very old tradition here. And great fun," he added.

Giovanni nodded to Luca, who took the Dowager's hand and led her towards one of the large wooden barrels.

"What are we doing?" she asked quietly through a smile.

"We go first."

"Oh, naturally," she agreed, though thoughts of murder were on her mind as a maid helped her tie up her skirts and washed her now slipper-and stocking-less feet. She was too proper to make a scene in public, and played along, murmuring, "I always wanted to tie my garters in public."

She had never felt a sensation quite so odd as the one she was now experiencing. She had never been allowed to run amok through open fields, mud and rivers as the boys had been allowed to do. She rarely was without slippers and found her feet to be extremely sensitive. It was what she would imagine stamping on insects would feel like. She had to force those thoughts from her mind and look at the grapes to remind herself she was not actually treading on anything alive. The villagers were cheering her on, and she was determined not to be a spoilsport. She smiled and kept on, not wanting to disappoint Luca.

He joined her in her barrel and attempted to twirl her around. This thrilled the onlookers, who were already in the spirit. She lifted her skirts a little higher and let Luca lead her about.

"What do you think?"

"It is very strange."

"But also invigorating."

"Indeed. And dizzying."

"What does that mean?"

"It means the world is spinning and I am about to go over the side of the barrel!" she laughed.

"Then we best stop. You have not even had any wine!"

He lifted her effortlessly and placed her in a tub of water for her feet to be cleaned. Once she was washed and put to rights, Luca led her away from the treading towards an area set aside for dancing.

"Shall we?" he smiled.

"We shall." She accepted his arm and the magic once again transformed them to that special place thirty-four years ago. When they danced, the rest of the world ceased to exist, except for the two of them, and it felt as if they were floating on air. The moon was rising full into the sky, and the heavenly sensation sent shivers up her spine. They stopped when they heard cheers, and looked about to see they had drawn a crowd.

"We have done it again."

"I did not notice them."

Luca gave the onlookers a quick nod of thanks and signalled for the music to continue. Other couples began dancing, including Gwen and Andrew. The Dowager and the Conte drew aside for drinks and watched people dance by.

"Gwendolyn has the bloom," Luca observed.

"Yes, I have always thought her exquisite."

"*Si*, but I mean the maternal bloom."

The Dowager took another look. "I do believe you are right. I wonder if she knows yet. I was beginning to think it might not be for them."

"They will want to be returning to England soon."

"After Christmas, I expect."

Luca tucked her arm in his. "Let us walk to the beach."

"Will we be missed?"

He looked at the crowd of jubilant dancers and grape-treaders. "I do not think so."

They walked quietly arm in arm down the path to the beach.

"One more dance?"

She nodded.

He held her tight in his arms and swayed back and forth. This dance was different.

"Luca?"

"You are going to leave again." It was a statement, not a question.

She paused before answering. "I think so." Her voice quivered. "I am not certain yet."

He remained silent.

"I have been alone too long now. When the newness wears off, you will regret having me around."

"Never!" he said under his breath, but did not let her go.

"It is inconceivable that you could still want me, Luca."

"I never stopped wanting you."

She looked away through her tears.

"Do not make me go on another day without you."

She continued to look away to control herself.

"Give us another chance."

He pulled her closer and whispered, "Choose for you this time. Choose me."

She let out a tiny sob.

"Where you go, I will follow. If you fall, I will catch you. If you are sad, I will wipe your tears. And when we are old, we will hold hands and hurt together. All I need is you. To be with you."

"Luca. I don't know what to say."

"Yes. Only yes. You will regret saying no. I can see it in your eyes."

"I'm…" the Dowager was interrupted.

"Father? *Duchessa?*" They heard Giovanni calling for them.

Luca's head fell onto her shoulder.

"*Si, figlio.*"

"Your presence has been requested. *Mi dispiace,*" he added apologetically.

"We will come."

Giovanni returned to the festivities. All Luca could say was, "Please don't leave me."

They walked in silence back to the square. The party was stopped and everyone had gathered around the fountain, where Andrew and Gwen stood next to Giovanni and Rosa.

"What is this?" Luca asked.

"We have a gift for you. A surprise." Giovanni handed Luca a wrapped package.

"*Aprilo!*" Rosa prodded excitedly.

Luca obeyed and looked as if he would faint when he saw the painting. He whispered, "*Mia bella.*" Tears came to his eyes. He set the painting down and walked away.

The four of them looked at the Dowager, who was staring at the painting as if she had seen as ghost.

"Gran? Are you ill?"

"I've made a horrible mistake," she whispered.

Andrew began to pull her away from the crowd. "Why don't we head back to the villa? I think we need to settle this in private."

Giovanni nodded and sent for their rides.

Andrew travelled beside the Dowager, with Gwen close behind. They said nothing until they were seated in the *salotto*.

"I had no idea the painting would upset everyone. I am very sorry," Gwen said regretfully.

"Do not be sorry, dear. You could not know. It is a beautiful painting. The mistake was mine."

"Why did it upset him so?" Rosa asked.

"I think because it showed the magic they make together. The love they have is in their eyes," Giovanni said with passion, trying to plead with the Dowager.

"But that is a beautiful thing," she protested.

Gwen had painted the Conte and the Dowager dancing in each other's arms and looking at each other. She had perfectly captured their love.

"But I have been blind and unable to see it. I was thinking of leaving again," Henrietta said wistfully.

"What can we do to help?" Gwen asked.

"I am afraid there is nothing you can do. Go ahead and prepare to leave. I need to find Luca."

"Do you know where he is?" Andrew asked.

"He has not come home yet," Giovanni said with concern.

"I have a couple of ideas," Henrietta said, thinking of the places they had frequented together the most.

"Do you wish for us to help you find him? It is dark outside."

"No. There is a bright moon. I prefer to go alone." The Dowager was adamant.

Andrew wanted to protest, but he felt a gentle pressure from his wife's hand and did not argue further.

HENRIETTA WAS AFRAID. She was repeating the same mistake again, and she had hurt him without intending to. She had not meant for him to think she was giving up completely, but they had been interrupted at the worst moment. She had not thought she was ready to commit, but that painting had opened her eyes. She had not realized how beautiful what they had together truly was. She was a complete and utter fool.

Now she must find him. She had to convince him she was in earnest and pray that she was not too late. She did not deserve him. How had she not known before? She had never been one to be indecisive. Why did it feel like there was so much more at stake now? She had always encouraged her children to take risks, and she was ignoring her own advice. She had nothing to lose except her heart. If she left now, she would be leaving it behind.

She first went to the orchard, but Luca was nowhere to be found. The moon was beginning to sink, and she was growing concerned. She eyed the path down to the beach and felt a moment's panic. She was probably going to fall and break her neck, but no, she could never do things the easy way. She wanted to close her eyes so she couldn't see how far down it was, but she forced that thought away and went one step at a time. She kept thinking about how good it had felt to be in Luca's arms as he'd carried her down here. God above, she was bewitched! Perhaps she should get on that boat and leave. He deserved better than her—someone who recognized a diamond when they held it in their hand.

Henrietta sat on a rock and let a rare moment of emotion overcome her. She was going to lose him. She probably already had. She had finally pushed him far enough away with her indecision that he saw how unworthy she was. When her tears stopped flowing, she realized she did not want to give up. She was a fighter, and she would only leave having fought her best fight. She wiped away her tears and forced herself to move on.

She finally made it to the beach. She was in awe of how different everything felt at night. The sea seemed fathomless, endless. She felt so small and vulnerable. She looked around, but there was no Luca. She had no idea where else to look. She saw the ship docked at the port that had come to take them away to France. The end had finally come.

Water crept over her feet as the tide began to come in. She needed to go back before she found herself swept away. But she did not want to go back alone. She had difficulty finding the path through the water, and struggled to climb. Rocks slid from under her feet several times, and she cursed herself for not wearing proper shoes. She had thought of nothing else save finding Luca when she had left the house.

She made it back onto the terrace breathless and exhausted. She felt she had aged twenty years tonight. The moon was low in the sky, looking like the one they had watched together that night when they had danced until dawn. She leaned over the railing to watch it one last time.

She looked up pleadingly toward the night, "Luca, come back to me."

"I was here the whole time," he said softly.

"Luca?" she gasped.

"*Si, mia bella* I'm here." He stood up from where he was sitting in the shadows along the railing and stood beside her.

"Did you know I was searching for you?"

"At first, no. I saw you leave and thought you wanted time alone to think as I did. Then, I wanted for you to search and find me. I knew if you could not see and feel what I did when you looked at that painting, then nothing I said or did was going to make you come back to me. You cannot force someone to return your love. I finally understood that tonight."

"Oh, Luca." She reached up and touched his cheek.

"Do you know how many nights I sat and watched the endless sea searching for answers?" he said as he looked into her eyes.

"Did it help?"

"Some. Mostly, I still thought of you and wondered if I would ever hold you again."

"You have me now."

"But for how long?"

"Until you tire of me and throw me into the sea."

He laughed. "That is more like it."

"Do you forgive me?"

"There is nothing to forgive. I told you."

"But there is. I have been blind and have hurt you. I do not want to hurt you, Luca. I love you."

"I know you love me. I have been waiting for you to realize it." He smiled.

"Will you hush and kiss me?"

"With pleasure."

EPILOGUE

The Italian coast faded from sight. Henrietta sighed. She already missed it. Saying goodbye was hard, but this time, it would not be forever.

"Why the sad face, *mia bella*? We will be back soon," Luca said as he placed his arms around her.

"I know. I think it might not be before the festival next year," she replied with a twinkle in her eye.

"Are you trying to avoid treading the grapes, my dear?" he teased.

"I think we should go to England until the baby comes," she reasoned.

"Of course, *mia bella*." He winked at her. "Perhaps we may return in time."

She harrumphed.

"When do you think Gwen will realize she is increasing?"

"She will when she doesn't feel any better on land. Right now, she believes she is seasick."

"*Comprendo.*"

"Do you think your family will mind that we did not wait to marry?"

"Most assuredly. But I wanted to be married in Italy, and I did not wish to make you wait another day."

"*Grazie.* I approve of your reasoning." He thanked her with a kiss.

"And Robert cannot try to change my mind."

"No, he cannot, *Contessa.*"

"I like the sound of that. Dowager made me feel old."

"Tell me about your family whom I am to meet in France. I hope they will like me better than your grandson did."

"You won Andrew over. You will be fine."

"*Si.* But I hope I will not be required to prove myself in so manly a fashion to each one." He laughed.

"I am the only one who matters."

"Not true. You matter the *most.*"

She smiled.

"You have met Robert. His wife is a stuffy prude. She has softened a little lately, but do not take her personally. She treats everyone with equal disdain."

"I cannot wait," he murmured.

"Their daughter is Beatrice. It is her home we are going to."

"Should we turn back?"

The Dowager cackled appreciatively. "No, she managed to overcome her upbringing, as did their son, Nathaniel." She paused reflectively. "He was injured severely in the war, but he does not let it hinder him. He will not wish to be treated any differently."

"Very well. I will remember."

"And,"

"There are more?" he interrupted.

"We cannot forget Elly. She is my pride and joy. You will understand when you meet her. She spent many years in America, but we have always remained close. She is my dear Elizabeth in the flesh. She has a very happy marriage and many children."

"I look forward to this one. Are there any others?"

Henrietta looked out over the sea sadly.

"There is one more, but she will not be there. Elizabeth's eldest child, Sarah."

"What happened to her?"

"She was deceived in her marriage. She will not discuss it. Her husband would not allow her to visit our family after they wed. She ran away to us one time, but he found her."

"There must be something that can be done."

"I am afraid not. All of the laws in England favour the husband. He owns her. Even Robert, a powerful duke, cannot intervene."

Luca muttered something unintelligible under his breath.

"Indeed."

"We must see how we can help when we go to England," he said passionately, and she gave his hand a thankful squeeze.

WHEN THEY ARRIVED IN FRANCE, the weather was as pleasant as it had been in Italy. Gwen had been ill the entire voyage and was ready to have some much-needed rest on a still bed. She looked green in the carriage ride from the port to the Vernon's Estate. Andrew was hovering over her protectively as Luca and Henrietta watched on with sympathy and amusement.

Henrietta was nervous again. She was happy with her decision, but she knew not all of her family members would be pleased.

The carriage pulled into the gates of the estate. Henrietta took several deep breaths, reminding herself to remain calm. When they alighted, the group of children playing nearby were deeply involved in a game of rounders, and their arrival was barely noticed.

Amelia waved and went back to concentrating on her next pitch.

"I'm glad I was nervous for nothing," Henrietta remarked.

Luca laughed. "It will be fine. Let us go find Robert and get it over with. I am not sure I am ready to meet all of the grandchildren at one time."

"I know I'm not," she retorted.

They proceeded into the house, which was equally as chaotic as the scene outside had been.

"What on earth is going on?" she demanded.

Beatrice heard her grandmother's voice and came running into the entry hall.

She ran to her and greeted her with a kiss. "Forgive me, Grandmama. There has been a fire in the kitchen and our chef has decided to leave in an uproar over it. He blamed the housekeeper, she blamed him, and he left. It is a long story, but our Christmas dinner is a disaster."

"That is the problem with French chefs. Their brilliance in the kitchen is only surpassed by their moods," Luca commented.

Beatrice laughed. "Indeed. And to whom do I have the pleasure of speaking with, Grandmama?" she looked at her grandmother with a smile.

"Oh, dear. I have failed already. This is my husband, the Conte de Salerno. Luca, meet my granddaughter, Beatrice, Lady Vernon."

"It is a great pleasure to meet you, Lady Vernon." He took her hand and kissed it.

"Your…your husband?" Beatrice looked at her grandmother questioningly.

"Yes." Henrietta smiled happily, but said no more.

"Well, welcome, sir. I suppose you two will not mind sharing an apartment if you are just married. As you can see we have quite a houseful."

"We do not mind," her grandmother reassured her with a slight blush.

"Come in and greet everyone. I'm sure they will be delighted with your news."

Beatrice led them into a parlour, which was crowded with people. "Look who has arrived. Grandmama has brought her new husband. May I present the Conte de Salerno."

The entire room grew silent and turned to stare.

The first to shut her jaw and greet them was Elly, who rushed toward them with her arms out.

"Oh, my goodness. Welcome, sir. Do you realize what you have married into?" she said with a sparkle in her eye.

He bowed low. "You must be Elly."

"Indeed." She smiled brilliantly at him. "I can see Grandmama has warned you about us." She tucked her arm in his. "Shall I introduce you around?"

"I would be delighted." He looked at his bride with an amused smile and followed Elly to meet the clan.

Henrietta walked toward Robert who looked contemplative.

"Hello, my son," she said as she reached his side.

"Hello, Mother. So you found each other again," he replied as he watched the Conte across the room.

"We did."

"I am happy for you. I have often looked back on that time and felt much guilt over my selfishness."

"Have you? I never knew."

"You gave up everything for us, but you never seemed unhappy."

"I made the best choice I could at the time. There was no point in making everyone else miserable too. At least we were given a second chance. It was more than I could have hoped for."

"Thank you," he said quietly.

"You are welcome, dear." She squeezed his hand in a rare exchange of emotion between the two.

She looked up and gasped. "Is that Sarah?" she whispered to Robert.

"Yes," he replied sadly.

"What has happened? I almost did not recognize her."

"She is finally free."

"Abernathy divorced her?" she said in shock.

"No, he has taken his place in hell."

Robert allowed his words to sink in before continuing. "He was killed in a duel by an irate husband. I am sad for the scandal, but once it dies down, it will be much better for everyone. Sarah and the children needed time away, so we brought them here."

Henrietta nodded and walked over to Sarah. She sat next to her and wrapped her arms around her granddaughter without a word. Sarah was skin and bones. Her skin was covered in a rash and deep circles surrounded her eyes. She began to weep in Henrietta's arms.

"I am so glad you're here. We have had too many Christmasses without you."

All Sarah could do was nod.

"Everything will be better soon, dear. I promise," Henrietta tried to reassure her.

When Sarah was able, she excused herself to her room.

Tea was brought in, and Beatrice brought up the dilemma of how Christmas dinner was to be saved.

"We normally give most of the servants the day off to be with their families. I hate to ask them to change their plans," she stated.

"I do not see a problem." Elly spoke. "You know how to cook, I know how to cook a little." She turned toward her sister-in-law. "Gwen?"

At the mention of food, Gwen rushed off to the nearest basin to be sick. Everyone had the same thought, but no one said a word.

"The problem is that the kitchen is burnt," Beatrice replied.

"Adam, Nathaniel, Rhys and Andrew can be useful as well. They learned to make their own fire and cook over it in the Army," Elly suggested.

"Yes, we all know how to cook Army rations. It will be delightful. Easton is good at fish, Andrew is decent at overcooking eggs, and Vernon excels at bartering for brandy," Nathaniel said dryly.

"I know how to make wine," the Dowager said helpfully.

The family stared at her.

"That will be helpful next year," Luca said humorously, at which everyone laughed.

Andrew walked in the room just as his cooking talents were being slandered.

"You don't think I can cook, Fairmont?" he challenged. "I think perhaps the men need to give the ladies a break and take over the cooking, seeing as my wife is too ill to say the word food."

"I feel a wager coming on," Vernon quipped.

"I'm staying out of this," Easton remarked as he shook his head.

"Oh, no, you don't," Andrew warned. "Each of us makes a dish, and the family chooses the winner."

"The winner gets what? Other than bragging rights, of course," Vernon asked.

"Isn't that enough?" Andrew asked in exasperation.

"Well, yes," Vernon said as he thought about it.

"Winner shall claim a forfeit," Andrew announced.

"Andrew will lose, and he has to name his firstborn after the winner," Nathaniel suggested.

"Doesn't Gwen get a say?" Bea intervened.

All the men turned to glare at her as if she were daft.

"Forget I asked," Bea held up her hands.

The men were quite satisfied with their challenge.

Elly spoke up, "You had best decide what you are to make. You do not have much time and you may need to send for ingredients."

A look of panic briefly crossed each of their faces. They had only ever had to deal with rations or with what they could hunt.

"It shall remain a surprise," Andrew announced.

As the ladies sat around pondering what their dinner would consist of, and if they would actually have anything edible, the men scrambled away to plot and prepare.

CHRISTMAS EVE ARRIVED. The kitchen had been made functional again, and each of the men had gathered their supplies and ingredients in secret. The children and ladies had seen to the decorating, and had to pull the men away from the kitchen long enough to fetch the Yule log.

When the ladies were seated at the table for Christmas dinner, they speculated with amusement on what they would be served.

"Does anyone have any clues?" Elly asked.

"None," Beatrice exclaimed. "The only thing I surmised was each person was doing a dish from different countries."

"I certainly hope Luca makes something from Italy," Henrietta said fondly.

"I have no idea what Easton is up to," Elly added.

"I pray the food is edible," Gwen said.

"I am certain Vernon's contribution will be some French wine and brandy," Beatrice laughed.

Lydia shook her hand. "I don't want your child to be named Nathaniel," she said to Gwen, whose eyes grew large. Lydia's hand flew to her mouth. "You didn't know?"

"I, I, no. I didn't." Tears formed in Gwen's eyes.

Lydia rushed over to give her a hug. "I am so sorry. I assumed you knew."

"Do not be sorry. These are tears of happiness. It has taken so long that I thought I wasn't meant to be a mother. I was afraid to hope I was sick for a good reason."

The other ladies gathered around Gwen to offer their congratulations. When the men entered carrying their dishes they stood there stupefied at the scene before them.

"This is anti-climactic," Nathaniel muttered.

"I had rather thought they would be waiting with bated breath," Andrew agreed.

"She has realized," Luca said with a smile, watching Gwen.

"Realized what?" Andrew asked.

"Why don't you ask her," Luca prodded.

Andrew looked worried, but he placed his dish of plum pudding on the table and walked over to his wife. "Is something amiss, darling?"

Gwen shook her head. "No. We are to have a baby, Andrew."

"A baby?" He looked worriedly over at his dish on the table and the men started laughing.

"Do not worry, we would not vote for your daughter to be named Nathaniel."

"I think this calls for a celebration," Vernon explained as he held his contribution to the meal in the form of drinks as his wife suspected he would.

Robert put his turkey on the table.

Nathaniel placed fresh loaves of bread.

Easton laid out dishes of fish.

Sir Charles added his mincemeat pies.

Luca set a steaming plate of lasagne before his wife, who looked on approvingly.

Some of the children came in behind with dishes of vegetables, fruits and cheeses, and the ladies were astonished.

"It looks edible!" Elly said in amazement.

"I did not think it would be anything like a Christmas dinner," Bea remarked.

"How did you manage to knead the bread, Nathaniel?" Lydia asked. He smiled and winked at Amelia.

"Let us taste everything!"

"First, let us give thanks for where we are today. It has been a long time since we have all been together as a family." He smiled at Sarah then looked toward Luca. "Would you do the honours?"

"I would be pleased to."

When the food had been blessed, Robert carved the bird, Luca served the lasagne, and the other dishes were passed until everyone had some.

"I think I like this way of celebrating Christmas," Andrew remarked.

"It is a nice tradition to start," Robert agreed.

"I don't know if I want to cook every year," Andrew pondered.

"Let us taste. We aren't sure if we want you to cook again either," Nathaniel added.

The food was eaten, and the men were anxious for a vote.

"How do we do this politely?" Beatrice asked.

"We don't."

"I would like to say, everyone's food is lovely, but my Luca's lasagne is impeccable," Henrietta said proudly.

Everyone had to agree.

"So do we pick the worst?" Andrew asked.

"There was no worst. Father had someone else cook his bird, Vernon didn't cook…" Nathaniel began.

"I object! This wine was crafted on the estate," Vernon defended.

"By you?" Nathaniel asked.

"Not precisely."

"I rest my case. Sir," he turned to Luca, "welcome to the family."

AFTERWORD

Author's note: British spellings and grammar have been used in an effort to reflect what would have been done in the time period in which the novels are set. While I realize all words may not be exact, I hope you can appreciate the differences and effort made to be historically accurate while attempting to retain readability for the modern audience.

Thank you for reading *Second Dance*. I hope you enjoyed it. If you did, please help other readers find this book:

1. This ebook is lendable, so send it to a friend who you think might like it so she or he can discover me, too.

2. Help other people find this book by writing a review.

3. Sign up for my new releases at www.Elizabethjohnsauthor.com, so you can find out about the next book as soon as it's available.

4. Come like my Facebook page www.facebook.com/Elizabethjohnsauthor or follow on Twitter @Ejohnsauthor or feel free to write me at elizabethjohnsauthor@gmail.com

ABOUT THE AUTHOR

Like many writers, Elizabeth Johns was first an avid reader, though she was a reluctant convert. It was Jane Austen's clever wit and unique turn of phrase that hooked Johns when she was 'forced' to read Pride and Prejudice for a school assignment. She began writing when she ran out of her favourite author's books and decided to try her hand at crafting a Regency romance novel. Her journey into publishing began with the release of Surrender the Past, book one of the Loring-Abbott Series. Johns makes no pretensions to Austen's wit, but hopes readers will perhaps laugh and find some enjoyment in her writing.

Johns attributes much of her inspiration to her mother, a former English teacher. During their last summer together, Johns would sit on the porch swing and read her stories to her mother, who encouraged her to continue writing. Busy with multiple careers, including a professional job in the medical field, writing and mother of small children, Johns squeezes in time for reading whenever possible.

PREVIEW OF THROUGH THE FIRE

Gavin looked at the letter in his hand in utter disbelief. His heart was tearing in two. His brother, wife, and children had been killed when their carriage had slipped down the side of a cliff.

"This canna be true." He shook his head and fought back tears.

"I'm afraid it is, my lord."

"My lord? No. I doona wish for it. I'm a simple country doctor. I have a humble life and practice here."

"I'm terribly sorry for your loss, my lord. But you are, in fact, the eleventh Baron Craig now, and thus have some rather large holdings that are your responsibility."

"This was not supposed to happen. Iain had three strapping young lads!"

The solicitor looked grave. "Perhaps, my lord, it would be best for you to return to Castle Craig and see for yourself."

The solicitor was met with a blank stare from a set of startling blue eyes; a look that was common to those who had been met with grievous news, but who had not yet assimilated the ensuing change in circumstances.

"Verra well. I'll join you there as soon as I have made arrangements."

Gavin went through the motions of closing up his house and seeing his practice into the capable hands of his apprentice from Lord Easton's school. He had taken many trips to England to the school in Sussex of late and had toyed with joining it as an instructor full time, but he had never been able to cut ties with Scotland. How would he practice medicine as Lord Craig? He would have to find a way, but he would also do his best to carry on with his brother's works in Parliament.

Gavin had seen more death than most, but he had not been prepared for the loss of his brother, or of Iain's wife and children. They had been the last family he'd had left. He'd never given a thought to running the large Castle Craig estate, and hoped desperately that his brother had appointed a trustworthy steward.

His carriage was loaded with immediate necessities. His servants would send the rest of his belongings with those of his staff who wished to join him at the new residence. He had one final stop before setting off to bury his brother and begin his new life.

He pulled through the gates of Alberfoyle Priory, one of Lord Vernon's estates that served as an orphanage. He had become attached to a family of children there; the boy was attending medical school, but the two girls were still in residence. It would pain him to leave these children more than anything else. In fact, since he had no family of his own, perhaps they would consider allowing him to adopt them.

"Dr. Craig!" Maili Douglas came running when she saw him and greeted him with a hug. She was promptly lifted off her feet into his arms.

"Hello, my love. Where is your sister?"

"In the sewing class."

"Would you be so good as to retrieve her? I would like to speak to you both."

The little girl wrinkled her forehead in concern, but then nodded and skipped off to find her sister. She returned with Catriona, who received the same welcome as her sister had.

"Hello, lass. You have grown again!"

"Am I not supposed to grow?"

"Indeed you are. Only not too fast." Gavin choked up as he thought of his three nephews who he would never see again, and who would never grow any older...

"Why are you sad, Dr. Craig?" Maili asked.

"I found out that my brother and his family have died."

"Like our mama and papa?" Catriona cocked her head up to look at him.

"Yes, lass. Just like that."

Catriona and Maili crawled into his lap to comfort him. "Are you all alone like us now?"

"I am, and that is part of what I wanted to speak to you about. I have to move away, and would not be able to see you as often."

"Please don't leave us!" the girls cried.

"I was hoping you would come with me—and Seamus, too, when he is home from school. Would you like that?"

"Would you be our new papa?" Catriona asked.

"I would adopt you, yes. But I will never try to replace your papa or mama."

The girls threw their arms around his neck.

"That would be perfect."

"I will return for you after I have arranged everything with your guardian and buried my brother."

"Must you leave us?"

"I am afraid so, but I will be back for you soon." He exchanged hugs with the girls and took his leave to go and bury his brother and his family.

Lady Margaux Ashbury had wanted to join a convent, but her parents had insisted she instead remove to their new orphanage north of Glasgow for a short repairing lease before doing something so drastic. She had been enamoured with Scotland when she had visited Lord

Vernon's estate while they were courting a few years back. Despite her less fortunate outcome, she still loved Scotland.

After Lord Vernon had married his true love instead, her family had attempted to divert her with trips to London and to the Continent after Napoleon was defeated. But she had come to the realization that she was content on her own. She had always been the most independent of her sisters, and decided that brilliant marriages could be left in their capable hands. She certainly preferred the spinster state to marrying for convenience. She found she was content helping with the orphans, though she did very little with the establishment's competent staff which her family had appointed.

"What are you pondering, *mon amie?*" Margaux heard her mother ask.

"Very little, *Maman,*" she remarked, as they sat darning socks for some of the children. Her parents had remained with her, hopeful to change her mind.

"We are having a guest for dinner tonight. Someone interested in contributing to the orphans."

"*Tres bien,*" she said absentmindedly. Guests were a normal occurrence with her parents.

"You should wear the emerald satin. Bring some colour to your face, *non?*"

"If you wish, *Maman.*" Margaux cared little for what she wore these days.

"*Nous allons.*" Lady Ashbury stood and directed her daughter to do the same. "I will see you at dinner."

Lady Margaux went through the motions of dressing. Her maid arranged her hair in a manner worthy of a ball, she noticed. She must admit she had been having a mild case of the dismals. Once she established a routine here she would come out of it, she was certain. She had never been one to sulk, but she needed to find something useful to occupy her time. No, she corrected her thoughts. To make a new life.

She made her way downstairs, determined to be more cheerful. If she could only convince her parents she was happy here, then they would be satisfied she was content.

"Ah, there she is now, Lord Craig," Lord Ashbury remarked.

"Dr. Craig?" Margaux said, stunned as she met the eyes of the handsome doctor who had been enamored of Lady Beatrice.

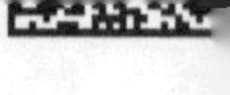